ONE HORSE
WAITING FOR ME

ONE HORSE
WAITING FOR ME

Patricia Mullins

Simon & Schuster Books for Young Readers

SIMON & SCHUSTER BOOKS FOR YOUNG READERS

An imprint of Simon & Schuster Children's Publishing Division

1230 Avenue of the Americas, New York, New York 10020

Copyright © 1998 by Patricia Mullins

First published in Australia in 1997 by Margaret Hamilton Books, a division of Scholastic Australia Pty Limited.

First American Edition, 1998.

SIMON & SCHUSTER BOOKS FOR YOUNG READERS is a trademark of Simon & Schuster.

The text for this book is set in 26 point Papyrus ICG.

The illustrations are collage made entirely from fine tissue and Japanese papers.

Printed and bound in Hong Kong

10 9 8 7 6 5 4 3 2 1

LC number 97-68018

To the equine heroes of my childhood:

Champion,
Pegasus,
Phar Lap,
Thowra,
and
Mr. Ed.

One horse waiting for me,

1

2

Two horses in the shade of a tree,

3

Three horses high in a cloud,

Four horses neighing out loud,

Five horses rolling along,

5

Six horses proud and strong,

6

Seven horses all shapes and sizes,

7

Eight horses wearing ribbons and prizes,

8

9

Nine horses rocking up and down,

Ten horses
going around and around,

Eleven horses in a sapphire sea,

12

Twelve horses . . .

running wild and free!